The telephone rang and Nancy picked up the receiver. "Hello?"

"Nancy, it's Riley!" a voice said. "I need your help!"

Nancy blinked. Riley sounded upset.

"What's wrong?" she asked.

"I heard you're a detective," Riley said. Her voice cracked. "And I need a detective because Martin is missing!"

Nancy was too surprised to speak.

"Martin . . . missing?" she finally gasped. "I'll be at your house first thing tomorrow morning, Riley."

"I don't get it, Chip," Nancy told her dog. She shook her head slowly. "Who would want to steal a *turkey*?"

The Nancy Drew Notebooks

Available from Simon & Schuster

THE NANCY DREW NOTEBOOKS®

#56

Turkey Trouble

CAROLYN KEENE
ILLUSTRATED BY JAN NAIMO JONES

Aladdin Paperbacks
New York   London   Toronto   Sydney   Singapore

This book is a work of fiction. Any references to historical events, real people, or real locales are used fictitiously. Other names, characters, places, and incidents are the product of the author's imagination, and any resemblance to actual events or locales or persons, living or dead, is entirely coincidental.

First Aladdin Paperbacks edition October 2003
Copyright © 2003 by Simon & Schuster, Inc.

ALADDIN PAPERBACKS
An imprint of Simon & Schuster
Children's Publishing Division
1230 Avenue of the Americas
New York, NY 10020

The text of this book was set in Excelsior.

Printed in the United States of America
10 9 8 7 6 5 4 3 2 1

NANCY DREW, THE NANCY DREW NOTEBOOKS, and colophon are registered trademarks of Simon & Schuster, Inc.

Library of Congress Control Number 2003103452

ISBN 0-689-85696-2

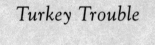

Turkey Trouble

1

Riley's Secret

Popcorn?" Nancy Drew asked in the school-yard. "At the first Thanksgiving?"

George Fayne's dark curls bounced as she nodded her head. "The Indians brought popped corn to the first Thanksgiving dinner," she said. "I read it in a book!"

"With all that popcorn," Bess Marvin said, "they probably went to the movies, too."

George rolled her eyes at her cousin. "News flash, Bess," she said. "There *were* no movies back then."

"I knew that!" Bess insisted. But she didn't look too sure.

Nancy smiled as she walked through the schoolyard before class with her two best friends. It was Friday and Thanksgiving was less than a week away!

"Guess what?" Nancy asked. She swung her backpack by its straps as she walked. "Hannah said she'd bake a pumpkin pie for me and Daddy on Thanksgiving."

"Yummy!" Bess exclaimed. "Hannah makes the best pies in River Heights."

Nancy thought so too. Hannah Gruen was the Drews' housekeeper. She had been living with them since Nancy's mother died when Nancy was only three years old.

"Hannah also wants to take us to a farm next Monday after school," Nancy added. "It's called 'Heavenly Harvest.'"

"A real farm?" Bess squealed.

Nancy nodded. "They have pumpkins, apple cider, a petting zoo—"

"Gobble, gobble, gobble!"

And turkeys? Nancy wondered. She spun around and saw Jason Hutchings, David Burger, and Mike Minelli. The boys were usually making trouble in Nancy's third-grade class at Carl Sandburg Elementary.

2

But this time they were making turkey sounds.

"Shh!" Jason placed a finger in front of his lips. "We're on a turkey hunt!"

"A turkey hunt?" Nancy asked.

"*Mr. Lizard's Funhouse* is having a Track a Turkey Contest!" Mike explained. "The first kid who brings a turkey to the TV station wins a bunch of neat prizes."

"And gets to dance the lizard dance on TV!" David added. "How cool is that?"

"Way cool," Nancy agreed. *Mr. Lizard's Funhouse* was her favorite TV show.

"I have an idea," Mike told Nancy. "Why don't *you* help us find a turkey? You're a detective, aren't you?" Mike asked. "And detectives are always great at finding things."

Nancy frowned. She was a detective. But she wasn't sure she wanted to help the boys find a turkey.

"Nancy has better things to do," George explained. She pointed at the boys. "Besides, I see three turkeys already!"

"Very funny!" Jason sneered.

The girls giggled as the boys walked away.

Nancy, George, and Bess started to talk about the farm again.

"I can't wait to see the animals in the petting zoo!" George exclaimed.

"I can't wait to pick pumpkins!" Nancy added excitedly.

"And I can't wait to wear my new corduroy jeans with the matching jacket," Bess said. "It's the perfect outfit for the farm!"

Nancy knew that Bess had a closet full of pretty clothes. But today all three girls were dressed for the chilly November weather. They wore parkas, scarves, mittens, and hats.

Suddenly someone tugged the pom-pom on the back of Nancy's hat. She spun around and saw eight-year-old Katie Zaleski.

Katie was in Mrs. Reynolds third-grade class just like Nancy, George, and Bess. But this morning she was standing with Emma Lindstrom, a girl in the fourth grade.

"Guess what, you guys?" Katie asked in an excited voice. "Emma asked me to join her new club!"

"What club?" Nancy asked. She saw an orange giraffe pin on Emma's parka. Katie wore a parrot pin on her own jacket.

"It's called 'Kids for Animals' and I'm president," Emma replied. "We believe all animals should be free. That means no birdcages, fish tanks, or dog leashes."

"But dogs have to be on leashes," Nancy pointed out. "It's the law."

"How do you know?" Emma demanded.

"I have my own puppy," Nancy answered. "She's a black Lab and her name is Chocolate Chip. She . . ."

Nancy's voice trailed off as Emma walked away.

"Don't worry, Nancy," Katie said. "Emma just likes to think she knows everything about animals."

"What's so great about that club anyway?" George wanted to know.

"Come to our meeting tomorrow and see for yourself!" Katie answered. "We meet every Saturday at three o'clock sharp."

Katie scribbled Emma's address in her notebook. Then she tore out the sheet and handed it to Nancy.

Nancy wasn't sure if she wanted to join Emma's club. But it was nice of Katie to invite them.

"Emma gave me my first club assignment this morning," Katie told them. "And I can't wait to carry it out."

"What do you have to do?" Bess asked.

"Can't tell!" Katie pretended to zip her lips. "It's a club secret!"

The school bell rang. Katie ran to catch up with Emma. Nancy, Bess, and George headed for the entrance.

As they lined up to go inside the school, Nancy noticed Riley McArthur, the new girl in their class. Riley was stepping out of her father's blue minivan in front of the school.

"Riley seems nice," Nancy said. "Maybe I'll invite her to the farm on Monday. She probably wants to make some new friends."

"Good idea," George agreed.

The girls watched as Mr. McArthur pulled a huge crate out of the van. It was covered with a thick blanket. He placed the crate on a wagon and wheeled it toward the school. Riley skipped after him.

"I wonder what *that* is!" Bess said.

"Who knows?" George said. "But I think we're going to find out soon."

The girls filed into Mrs. Reynolds's classroom. Nancy saw their friend Rebecca Ramirez inside. It was Rebecca's turn to clean the hamster cage. Riley was there too. So was the mysterious crate. It stood on the floor in front of the chalkboard.

"Whatever's in there smells funny," Amara Shane said, squeezing her nose.

"It's making noises, too," Orson Wong said excitedly. "Maybe Riley kidnapped an alien from some weird planet!"

Nancy wished she could see through the blanket. What was underneath?

"Class," Mrs. Reynolds announced, "Riley has brought something in to show us. And just in time for Thanksgiving!"

Brenda Carlton marched to the front of the classroom. "But Mrs. Reynolds!" she complained in a snooty voice. "I wanted to show my new laptop computer today!"

"Sorry, Brenda," Mrs. Reynolds said. "But Riley's surprise can't wait."

"Who cares about Riley?" Brenda grumbled as she plopped behind her desk.

Nancy wasn't surprised. She knew how nasty Brenda could be sometimes.

"Okay, Riley," Mrs. Reynolds said with a

smile. "Show us what you brought."

Riley yanked the green blanket off the crate. Everyone gasped. Underneath was a live turkey inside a cage. "Ta-daa!" she announced. "Meet Martin!"

Nancy brushed aside her reddish blond bangs so she could see everything. Martin's feathers were mostly brown and gray. He had a black fuzzy beard on his chest with a red feather in the middle.

"Cool!" David called out. "How did you get a real, live turkey?"

"My aunt and uncle own a farm," Riley explained. "They lent me Martin for show-and-tell today."

Excited whispers filled the classroom. Riley unhooked the cage door. She pulled a few corn kernels from her pocket and held them out. Martin stepped out and pecked at the corn.

"Eww!" Brenda cried. "Turkeys are yucky. I wouldn't have one in my house!"

"She's just jealous!" Bess whispered to Nancy.

"Are there any questions for Riley?" Mrs. Reynolds asked the class.

"Gobble, gobble!" Martin screeched. He flapped his wings and began racing through the classroom.

"Gobble, gobble, gobble!"

Nancy gasped as Martin brushed past her legs. But the turkey wasn't the only creature on the run. The class hamster had escaped from its cage too!

"Martin is chasing the hamster!" Molly Angelo cried.

"No!" Kyle Leddington shouted. "The hamster is chasing Martin!"

"Wild turkey!" Orson yelled. "Wild turkey on the loose!"

2

Gobble Gobble—
Trouble!

"**G**obble, gobble, gobble!" Martin cried. His wings flapped as he darted up and down the aisles. The little hamster scurried under the desks and the chairs.

Everyone except Brenda chased the animals through the classroom.

"Gotcha!" Riley yelled. She wrapped her arms around Martin's big feathery body.

Seconds later George scooped up the hamster and put him back in his cage.

"Rebecca?" Mrs. Reynolds asked. "Did you forget to latch the door on the hamster cage this morning?"

Rebecca's dark eyes looked worried.

"I must have left it open by mistake," she said slowly. "Sorry, Mrs. Reynolds."

Using more corn kernals, Riley led Martin back into his cage. She shut the door and latched it.

"Is that gross thing going to be here all day?" Brenda complained.

"My dad is picking Martin up during lunch," Riley explained. "First Martin is going to my house, then back to the farm."

"Will he be in a *cage*?" Katie asked.

"Martin is kept in a pen at the farm," Riley said. "With other animals."

"A pen?" Katie gasped. "But Martin should run free!"

"Duh!" Jason groaned. "He just did."

"Okay, kids," Mrs. Reynolds said. "Let's thank Riley for bringing Martin to class. Then take out your math workbooks."

Riley smiled as everyone called out their thanks.

"This was the best show-and-tell since Orson brought in his grandmother's false teeth!" Kyle declared.

Nancy was happy for Riley. She would have lots of friends soon!

Martin sat quietly in his cage all morning. At lunchtime Mr. McArthur came to pick him up.

Nancy and her friends watched from the window over their lunch table.

"There goes Martin now," Nancy said. She could see Mr. McArthur wheeling the cage to his car. Riley stood in the schoolyard waving good-bye.

"If you ask me, Riley McArthur is a big show-off," Brenda scoffed.

"And *I'm* a big loser!" Rebecca sighed. "How could I forget to lock the hamster cage? How?"

Nancy looked up from the egg salad sandwich she was unwrapping. "It was an accident, Rebecca," she said.

"I know," Rebecca sighed. "But—"

"Free Martin now!" Emma's shouting voice interrupted. "Free Martin now!"

"Free *Martin*?" Nancy asked. She turned her head and saw Emma and Katie. They were walking over to their table.

"Read this!" Emma said. She looked serious as she handed each girl a paper. Nancy studied the paper. It had a drawing of a turkey on it. Underneath was the slogan FREEDOM FOR MARTIN!

"Freedom from what?" Nancy asked.

"His *cage!*" Emma replied. "Katie told me Martin was stuck in there all morning."

"A *stinky* cage!" Brenda added.

"But Martin's a bird!" George said. "And Katie keeps her parrot, Lester, inside a cage sometimes. Right Katie?"

"I . . . um," Katie gulped.

"Is that true?" Emma demanded.

"Only when I take him to the vet!" Katie blurted out. "Or in my mother's car!"

Nancy watched as Emma waved Katie on to the next table.

"I can't believe Katie likes that club," Bess said. "Emma seems so bossy."

"Let's hide the papers before Riley sees them," Nancy suggested. "They might hurt her feelings."

Everyone slipped the papers under Nancy's backpack just as Riley came over.

"Hi!" Riley said. She was carrying her lunch in a bag. "May I eat with you?"

"Sure!" Nancy said cheerily. "There's a chair right next to Brenda."

Brenda grabbed her laptop computer and placed it on the empty chair. "Sorry!" she said nastily. "I'm saving this chair for my best friend, Alison Wegman!"

"Alison is out sick," Bess said.

"So what?" Brenda argued. "She might feel better and decide to come in."

"Not fair, Brenda!" George scolded. "That seat is empty and you know it."

"It's okay," Riley blurted out. "I'll sit at the other table. I don't mind."

Everyone watched in silence as Riley walked to the next table.

That does it, Nancy thought. *Now I really want to be friends with Riley!*

"Hey, kids," Mr. Lizard said on television. "Next week is Thanksgiving, so get ready to gobble down all that food!"

"Gobble—like a turkey!" Nancy laughed out loud. "I get it!"

"Cute," Hannah chuckled as she walked into the den. "But dinner will be ready in ten minutes. So go upstairs and wash up."

"Can I do the lizard dance first, Hannah?" Nancy asked. Her puppy, Chip, barked as

Nancy jumped up and wiggled her fingers behind her head.

Mr. Lizard always ended his show with the lizard dance. But this time he flapped his arms and strutted like a turkey. Nancy followed along.

"My birdwatchers club has spotted lots of different birds in River Heights," Hannah said. "But we never saw a turkey."

"I saw one in school today," Nancy said happily. "And his name was Martin!"

Hannah smiled and left the den. The telephone rang and Nancy picked up the receiver. "Hello?"

"Nancy, it's Riley!" a voice said. "I got your number from the class telephone list and I need your help!"

Nancy blinked. Riley sounded upset.

"What's wrong?" she asked.

"I heard you're a detective," Riley said. Her voice cracked. "And I need a detective because Martin is missing!"

Nancy was too surprised to speak.

"Martin . . . missing?" she finally gasped.

"My aunt and uncle were supposed to pick him up tomorrow morning," Riley explained. "But his cage and wagon disappeared from my yard this afternoon!"

"Oh, no!" Nancy cried. She felt sorry for Riley and wanted to help her.

"I'll be at your house first thing tomorrow morning, Riley," Nancy offered.

"Cool!" Riley said. She sounded relieved. "Can you bring Bess and George to my house too?"

"Sure," Nancy said. "Bess and George always help me with my cases."

Riley gave Nancy her address. "See you tomorrow. Bye, Nancy," she said.

Nancy hung up the phone. She was totally stunned. She had just seen Martin that morning in class!

This doesn't look good, Nancy thought. *If Martin's whole cage and wagon are gone, then he must have been stolen!*

"I don't get it, Chip," Nancy told her dog. She shook her head slowly. "Who would want to steal a *turkey*?"

3

Members Only

"Can I see your detective notebook?" Riley asked Nancy. "Do you really record every case?"

"Yes, I do," Nancy said. She took out her notebook and showed it to Riley.

"Cool!" Riley said.

It was Saturday afternoon. Nancy, Bess, and George stood with Riley in her backyard.

"Now, let's get to work," Nancy suggested. "Riley, where was Martin's cage before it disappeared?"

"Over there!" Riley said. She pointed to a

corner of the yard. Nancy, Bess, and George searched the area for clues.

"Found something!" Bess called. She held up a small silver object.

Nancy studied the item. It was a silver pin shaped like a cow.

"I never saw that in my life," Riley insisted. "I don't even like cows!"

"If you've never seen it, then it's a clue," Nancy said to Riley. "Maybe this pin belongs to whoever stole Martin." She dropped the pin into her parka pocket.

Riley followed the girls as they looked around the yard. Nancy noticed a tall fence surrounding the backyard.

"It would be hard to lift the cage and wagon over that fence," Nancy decided.

She looked down and saw tracks in the dirt. They looked like wheel tracks.

"Whoever wheeled Martin away," Nancy thought out loud, "wheeled him around the house to the front."

"You mean right past the house?" George asked, surprised. She turned to Riley. "No one in your house saw anything?"

"No!" Riley answered. "We must have been busy."

"It's possible," Nancy said. She opened her notebook and turned to a clean page. First she wrote the words "cow pin." Next she drew a picture of the wagon tracks and the house.

"Two clues already!" Riley exclaimed. "What do we do next?"

"We usually discuss the case," Nancy replied.

"Cool!" Riley exclaimed. "Can we discuss it over ice-cream sundaes?"

Nancy, Bess, and George smiled.

"Good idea, Riley!" Nancy said. "We're going to like working with you!"

All four girls got permission and rode their bikes to the Double Dip ice-cream parlor on Main Street. Once inside they ordered gooey sundaes and bubbly sodas.

Nancy swallowed a spoonful of chocolate fudge. Then she carefully opened her notebook on the table.

"Let's start a suspect list," Nancy suggested. "Who would want to steal—"

Splat! A green worm covered with gooey brown stuff landed on Nancy's notebook.

"Eeeek!" Bess shrieked.

"It's not real!" George said. She flicked the squiggly thing off the page. "It's a *candy* worm!"

Nancy spun around and looked straight at Lonny and Lenny Wong. They were sitting at the next table with their mother.

"We're eating Creepy Crawly Sundaes!" Lonny called to the girls. "It's ice cream covered with gummy worms!"

"Who are they?" Riley whispered.

"Lonny and Lenny are Orson's six-year-old twin brothers," Bess whispered back. "They're *double* trouble!"

"Boys!" Mrs. Wong scolded the twins. "Don't ever throw your food again. And don't talk with your mouths full either."

Nancy didn't like the messy chocolate spot in her notebook, so she flipped to a fresh page. "Let's try again." She sighed. "Who would want to steal a turkey?"

"Maybe someone from our class," Bess said. "Who else would know about Martin?"

"What about Brenda?" George asked. She

licked marshmallow sauce from her spoon. "She was mad at Riley for bumping her from show-and-tell."

"It can't be Brenda," Riley said. "Brenda thinks turkeys are yucky. She didn't even want to go near Martin."

Nancy's eyes lit up as she remembered something. "How about Jason, David, and Mike?" she asked. "They needed a turkey to win Mr. Lizard's Track a Turkey Contest!"

"And they'd do anything to get one too!" George added.

Nancy wrote "Jason, David, and Mike" in her notebook. But something didn't add up.

"What about the cow pin? The boys never wear pins," Nancy said. "Just those Mole-heads from Mars buttons. The ones that say 'You're a Space Cadet.'"

Just then the door of the ice-cream parlor swung open. Emma and Katie walked inside.

Instead of ordering ice cream they began tacking papers on the bulletin board.

"Hey," Nancy whispered. "Maybe the Kids for Animals Club let Martin out of his cage. Didn't Emma want to free him?"

"Wait a minute," Riley said. "Emma was planning to set Martin free? Why didn't anyone tell me?"

"We thought you might get upset if you knew. We didn't want to hurt your feelings," Nancy said.

"But we should have told you, since it is *your* case. We're sorry, Riley," George apologized.

"It's okay," Riley said, taking a big bite of her sundae.

"So, how can we find out if the Kids for Animals members know anything about Martin?" Bess asked. "They are so secretive."

"There's a meeting later at three o'clock," Nancy said. "Katie invited us. Remember?"

"Yeah!" George said. "Let's go there and see what we can find out."

"My first club meeting in my new neighborhood!" Riley cheered. She gave two thumbs-up signs. "All riiiight!"

Nancy, Bess, and George stared at Riley.

"Um, sorry, Riley," Nancy said. "If the club members see you at the meeting, they may not want to talk about Martin."

Riley looked disappointed at first. Then

she smiled. "It's okay," she said. "We'll do other fun stuff."

Fun? Nancy wondered. *I thought Riley was* upset *about Martin.*

"Nancy?" Bess interrupted her thoughts. "You don't think Katie took Martin, do you?"

"If she did," Nancy said, looking across the room, "I'm sure Emma had something to do with it."

Emma turned from the bulletin board and began to shout, "Free the snakes from the pet store! Free them *now*!"

"Snakes?" Bess shuddered. "I'm not sure I want to go to that meeting!"

"What are you doing here?" Emma asked after she opened her door.

Nancy, Bess, and George smiled as they stood on the Lindstroms' doorstep at three o'clock wearing animal pins on their jackets. Nancy had borrowed a rhinestone cat from Hannah. Bess wore a pretty butterfly pin. George didn't have a real pin, so she fastened a rubber spider to her shirt.

"Katie invited us to a meeting, Emma,"

Nancy said brightly. "If we like it, maybe we'll all join."

"Hold on just a minute!" Emma warned. "In order to become members you have to answer three questions about animals."

"Sure," Nancy said with a shrug.

"We like animals!" Bess added.

Emma led the girls to her bedroom, where the meeting had already started. Katie looked very happy to see them.

Nancy, Bess, and George sat on the floor with the others. Emma shut the door.

"First question," Emma said. "Do bulls run in flocks, gaggles, or herds?"

"Herds!" George called out.

The other club members nodded in approval. George was correct!

"Next question," Emma said. "What is a baby lion called?"

"A cub!" Nancy answered. She exchanged high fives with Bess and George.

"If you answer the last question, you're in the Kids for Animals Club," Emma said. "What do they call a female sheep."

Nancy gulped. She didn't know the

answer. And Bess and George didn't seem to know either. What were they going to do?

Nancy's eyes darted around the room. One girl yawned loudly as she waited for their answer. A boy reached into his pocket and pulled out a tiny pet snake!

Bess must have seen it because she let out a loud, "Ewwwww!"

"That's it!" Emma declared. "A female sheep is called a 'ewe.' So you're in!"

Nancy, Bess, and George sighed with relief. Now they could get to work!

"Are there any questions before we start the meeting?" Emma asked everyone.

"Yes!" Nancy said. She pulled out the silver cow pin. "Did anyone lose this?"

The kids shook their heads as they passed around the pin.

"We only answer questions about animals," Emma complained. "That was a question about animal *pins*. Any others?"

"What was the last animal you all freed from its cage?" George called out.

"I freed an animal yesterday," Katie said. "But I don't want to talk about it." Nancy stared at Katie. *Why wouldn't she talk about it? Could Martin be the animal she'd set free?*

"Then let's talk about freeing the ants from Kyle Leddington's ant farm," Emma suggested. "Any ideas?"

Most of the kids raised their hands.

Then suddenly strange noises came from outside Emma's room.

"Gobble, gobble, gobble."

Nancy's eyes opened wide. Something right outside Emma's door was gobbling—like a *turkey*!

4

Stakeout!

Omigosh! Did you hear that noise?"
Nancy whispered to Bess and George.

"How are we going to leave the meeting
and check it out?" Bess replied quietly.

George's hand shot in the air. "Um—excuse
us, Emma," she said. "But we think we
heard our bikes fall over outside!"

Before Emma could speak, the three
friends were out the door and in the hall.

"Gobble, gobble, gobble!"

"There it is again!" Nancy said. She followed the gobbling to a table standing in
the hall. It was covered with a long white

tablecloth. "If it is a turkey, he's under that table!"

George kneeled and stuck her hand under the tablecloth. "I feel feathers!" she exclaimed.

Nancy smiled. It had to be Martin!

"*Ow!*" George cried. She yanked back her hand. "He just pecked me!"

"Bad turkey!" Bess scolded.

Nancy lifted the tablecloth. But instead of finding Martin, she saw Katie's parrot, Lester!

"Lester?" Nancy, Bess, and George asked at the same time.

"Gobble, gobble!" Lester squawked. "Arrrk!"

The club members ran out of Emma's room into the hall.

"What's going on?" Emma asked.

Nancy pointed to Lester strutting out from under the table. "What's Lester doing here?" she asked.

"Lester goes everywhere with me, Nancy," Katie explained. "You know that."

"Then why is he out in the hallway

gobbling like a turkey?" George asked, wrinkling her nose.

"He's been doing that ever since he heard Mr. Lizard gobble on TV," Katie said. "Parrots repeat what they hear!"

"So what's the big deal?" Emma asked Nancy, Bess, and George.

"We thought Lester was Riley's turkey, Martin," Bess said. "He's been missing since yesterday."

"Missing?" Emma gasped.

Everyone else seemed surprised too.

"You said you freed an animal, Katie," Nancy reminded. "Was that animal Martin, the turkey?"

"No way!" Katie declared. "I did free an animal but it wasn't him."

"Then who was it?" Nancy asked.

Katie stared at her sneakers. "The class hamster," she said in a small voice.

"The hamster?" Nancy squeaked. She remembered the hamster running through the classroom yesterday.

"It was my first club assignment," Katie explained. "But I'm sorry I did it!"

"Why?" Emma asked.

"Because Rebecca was blamed for something I did!" Katie said. "And I'm going to tell Mrs. Reynolds on Monday."

"But you *have* to do things like that to be in my club!" Emma argued.

Katie placed her hands on her hips. "Then I don't want to be in your club anymore," she said firmly.

Emma frowned, but Nancy smiled. She was proud of Katie for sticking up for herself. Then Lester began to screech, "Emma is bossy! Emma is bossy! Raaaak!"

Emma's face turned red. "Parrots repeat what they hear, huh?" she said. "So that must be what Katie said about me!"

"Gotta go," Katie blurted out.

Nancy, Bess, George, and Katie ran down the stairs and out of Emma's house. Lester flapped after them.

"Who needs them?" Katie scoffed. "I already joined a better club—the River Heights Birdwatchers Brigade!"

Katie reached into her pocket and pulled out a small book. It had a picture of a robin on the cover.

34

"They gave me this guidebook and there's a whole page about turkeys!" she said. "You can borrow it if you'd like."

"Gobble, gobble!" Lester squawked.

Katie placed Lester on her shoulder and handed Nancy her guidebook. She gave a little wave and headed home.

"I'm glad Katie didn't free Martin," Nancy said. She crossed "Kids for Animals" out of her notebook. "But if the club didn't free Martin, then who dropped that cow pin in Riley's yard?"

"Did you know that only boy turkeys gobble, Daddy?" Nancy asked the next day at breakfast. "And that girl turkeys make clicking sounds instead?" Nancy was telling her dad about her latest case.

Carson Drew placed another stack of buckwheat pancakes on the table. He always made pancakes for Nancy on Sundays.

"Where did you learn all about turkeys, Pudding Pie?" Mr. Drew asked. Pudding Pie was his special nickname for Nancy.

"In Katie's birdwatcher booklet," Nancy explained. "I also learned that most boy turkeys have black fuzzy feathers on their chests. Just like Martin."

"Good work, Nancy," Mr. Drew praised. "Facts are very important in every case."

Nancy smiled at her father. He was a great lawyer. And a pretty good cook, too!

The doorbell rang. Nancy excused herself as she jumped up from her chair.

"That must be Bess, George, and Riley, Daddy," she said. "We're supposed to spend all day looking for Martin."

But when Nancy flung open the door, she didn't find her friends. Instead she found a note on her doorstep. It read:

Dear Detective Drew,

We have the turkey. Leave two bags of Crunchy Munchies and three cherry lollipops under the park slide today and you'll get him back.

P.S. Drop off the candy at noon—when both hands are on the twelve.

"Ohmigosh!" Nancy gasped. Her hands shook as she held the note. "This person knows where Martin is!"

When Bess, George, and Riley arrived, they studied the note together. It was written on plain white paper with brown, red, and orange crayon.

"Turkey colors!" Riley declared.

"Whoever has Martin likes candy," Bess pointed out.

"Everybody we know likes candy," George sighed. "It could be *anyone*!"

Nancy studied the note. "It says '*we* have the turkey,'" she pointed out. "So there's more than one turkey thief."

"How about *three* turkey thieves?" George asked. "Jason, David, and Mike?"

Nancy folded the note and slipped it in the pocket of her jeans. "There's only one way to find out," she said. "We'll have to catch the thieves candy-handed!"

"Like a stakeout?" Riley squealed. "This is going to be so much fun!"

Nancy watched Riley jump up and down. Maybe she was having *too* much fun.

"Come on," Nancy told the girls. "Let's fill up that candy bag."

Nancy still had candy left over from Halloween. They filled a brown paper bag with Crunchy Munchies and three cherry lollipops. When they reached the park they checked their watches.

"Five minutes to noon," Nancy said in a hushed voice. "All systems go."

First George tossed the candy bag under the slide. Next they ran and kneeled behind a bench. Nancy and her friends peeked out between the wooden slats.

"Any second now," Nancy whispered.

But instead of seeing the turkey thieves, the girls saw Hannah. She was walking toward the bench with two other grown-ups. They were all holding binoculars.

"It's Hannah and the River Heights Birdwatcher's Brigade!" Nancy said.

"Feeling lucky today?" Hannah was asking the man and woman.

"You bet, Hannah!" the man replied. "I'm going to keep my eyes peeled for a golden-cheeked warbler!"

"And a purple finch!" the woman added. "I love those purple finches!"

Nancy groaned as the three sat down on the bench. They were totally blocking the girls' view of the slide!

"Well, hi, Nancy!" Hannah said as Nancy, George, and Bess darted out from behind the bench.

Nancy stared at the space under the slide. The candy was gone—and so were the turkey thieves!

5
Fowl Play

Hi, Hannah," Nancy said, turning toward the grown-ups. She smiled politely at the other birdwatchers. Then she and her friends charged to the slide.

"I can't believe we missed them!" Nancy complained. "It happened so fast!"

They studied the black rubber mat under the slide. There were too many sneaker prints on it to know which belonged to the turkey thieves.

"If the turkey thieves have the candy," Bess said, "maybe they'll give Martin back!"

"Maybe," Riley said. "But in the meantime, let's go on the swings!"

"The swings?" George cried. "Don't you want to find Martin?"

"Sure I do!" Riley said. "But even detectives take breaks. Right, Nancy?"

Nancy was about to answer when a voice called out, "Hi, guys!"

It was Katie. She had binoculars around her neck and a smile on her face. "It's my first birdwatcher meeting," she said. "And I already spotted a cardinal!"

"While you were looking at birds," Nancy asked Katie, "did you see anyone running under the slide?"

Katie scrunched her eyebrows as she thought. "Just some boys," she said. "But I don't remember how many. Or what they looked like. They were too fast."

"Boys!" George repeated. She narrowed her eyes. "Like David, Jason, and Mike."

"If this is about Martin, good luck," Katie said. She held up her binoculars. "And if I spot a turkey in the park, I'll let you know."

Katie began making chirping sounds as she walked away.

"If the boys took Martin, they wouldn't give him back," Nancy decided. "They would need him in order to win Mr. Lizard's Track a Turkey Contest."

"Which means Martin could be at the TV station already," Bess said. "We should go there and find out."

"Wow!" Riley exclaimed. "I was never in a real TV station before!"

On the way out of the park the girls saw Lonny and Lenny Wong. This time their cheeks were puffed out like balloons.

"Are you eating gummy worms again?" Nancy asked.

The twins kept their mouths shut tightly as they shook their heads.

"Oh, I get it," George said. "Your mom told you not to talk with your mouths full, right?"

With their mouths still shut the twins nodded. As they scampered away Nancy had a thought.

"Do you think Lonny and Lenny were eating the candy we put under the slide?" Nancy asked.

"They're always eating something," Bess said. "But whoever ate the candy also left the note on Nancy's doorstep. The twins couldn't have written that note. They're only six."

Nancy, Bess, George, and Riley walked to station WRIV on Main Street. That's where Mr. Lizard did his show every week.

The girls filed through the spinning doors into the lobby. A woman sat behind a desk. Her nameplate read VIVIAN POTTS.

"Hello," Nancy said. "We'd like to—"

"Oh!" Ms. Potts cut in. "You must be the three lucky contest winners!"

Nancy opened her mouth to say no, but Ms. Potts cut in again.

"Your dad brought the turkey here this morning," she said. "What a big fella! Would you like to check up on him?"

"Yes, thank you!" George blurted out.

Nancy didn't want to pretend to be someone she wasn't. But she had to find out about Martin!

"All right then!" Ms. Potts said cheerily. She pointed down the hall. "The turkey is right behind that red door."

"Thank you!" the girls said at the same time. Then they raced down the hall.

"Did she really say there was a turkey

here?" Riley whispered in a puzzled voice.

"Yes!" Nancy whispered back. "And I'll bet it's Martin!"

Nancy pushed the red door open. The girls bumped into each other as they squeezed into the room.

"This is Mr. Lizard's dressing room!" Nancy said. There were racks of costumes and a row of bright red wigs on a table.

"But where's Martin?" George asked.

Nancy's eyes darted around the room. She saw a big square object in the corner. It was covered with a green blanket.

Nancy lifted the blanket and squealed. Underneath it was a cage. And inside the cage was a turkey!

"Is it Martin?" Nancy asked Riley.

"I don't know," Riley said. "I can't get a good look."

"I'll look inside," Nancy offered. She unlatched the cage door and opened it. She kneeled down and peeked into the cage.

"That's funny," Nancy said. "This turkey doesn't have a black beard."

"Maybe Martin shaved for the show tomorrow," Bess said.

Nancy leaned farther into the cage. But then the dressing room door swung open.

"Hey!" an angry voice shouted.

Nancy glanced over her shoulder. Jason, David, and Mike marched into the room and they looked mad!

"Help!" Mike shouted. "She's stealing our turkey! She's stealing our turkey!"

6

Truth in the Tooth

I was not stealing this turkey, Mike Minelli!" Nancy argued.

Mr. Lizard hurried into the room. He was tugging at the bright red wig on his head. "What's going on in here?" he asked.

"They were stealing our turkey, Mr. Lizard!" Mike said, pointing to Nancy. "We won the contest fair and square!"

"We weren't stealing, Mr. Lizard," Nancy said. "We just wanted to know if the boys stole Martin."

"Who's Martin?" Mr. Lizard asked.

"Martin is my turkey," Riley answered. "He's . . . missing."

"No way did we steal Riley's turkey," Mike said. He pointed to the cage. "My dad borrowed that one from a turkey farm."

"His name is Tommy," David added. "We named him ourselves."

"Wow!" Mr. Lizard said. He grinned at the turkey. "That's some gobbler, boys. He does gobble, doesn't he?"

"Not really," Mike admitted. "He just makes a weird clicking noise."

Clicking noise? Nancy remembered what she had read in Katie's bird booklet. Girl turkeys don't gobble, they make clicking noises. And many girl turkeys don't have beards, either.

"That's because Tommy the turkey is a girl turkey!" Nancy announced.

Everyone stared at Nancy.

"Is not!" Mike snapped.

"Is too!" Nancy snapped back.

"Is not!" Mike argued.

"Is too!" Nancy argued back.

"Is too," Mr. Lizard sighed. "Tommy just laid an egg."

Everyone stared into the cage. The turkey was standing over a big white egg!

"Give me a break," Mike muttered.

"A turkey's a turkey!" Mr. Lizard said. He reached out and shook each boy's hand. "And you boys just won the Track a Turkey Contest!"

"Cool!" Jason cheered.

Mr. Lizard kneeled down and stuck his head into the cage. "And congratulations to you—"

"Click, click, click!" The turkey stretched her neck out and plucked the wig right off Mr. Lizard's head!

"Hey!" Mr. Lizard shouted. He grabbed his bright red wig back.

Nancy tried hard not to giggle.

"First kids, and now animals!" Mr. Lizard grumbled as he left the room.

"I didn't know Mr. Lizard was bald," Riley said slowly.

"And I didn't know our turkey was a girl!" Mike groaned.

Nancy knew the boys didn't steal Martin. But they still could have written the mysterious note just to make trouble.

How can I find out? Nancy wondered.

Suddenly she had a brainstorm. Nancy

pulled out her notebook and a pen. She opened to a clean page and held it out.

"Can I have your autographs?" Nancy asked the boys. "Pleeeease?"

Bess, George, and Riley looked confused. So did the boys.

"What for?" Jason asked.

"You're going to dance the lizard dance on TV tomorrow," Nancy answered. "So you're going to be famous!"

The boys puffed out their chests proudly. One at a time they took the pen and signed Nancy's notebook.

"Just one autograph," David said in a snooty voice. "We're wanted on the set!"

"Thanks," Nancy forced herself to say. She pulled out the mysterious note and compared it with the boys' signatures. They did not match.

"What are you doing now?" Mike asked.

"Just clearing you from this case," Nancy explained. "But do us a favor."

"What?" the three boys asked.

"Change Tommy's name," Nancy said, giggling, "to Tomasina!"

The boys turned red as the girls left the room. Once outside Nancy crossed their names out in her notebook.

"We still don't know who wrote the note," Nancy said. "Hopefully they'll write again and we'll get more clues."

"What should we do in the meantime?" George asked.

"I know!" Riley said. "Let's go to the movies. Or ice-skating! Or bowling!"

Nancy stared at Riley as she did cartwheels down the block.

"What's with Riley?" Nancy asked. "It's like she's not worried about Martin anymore."

Bess put her arm around Nancy's shoulder. "That's because *you're* on the case, Nancy," she said with a smile.

"Sure," George agreed. "If anyone can find a missing turkey, it's you!"

"Thanks," Nancy said. But she was getting worried. Finding a missing turkey was a lot harder than she thought.

The girls were getting hungry. So they each decided to go to their houses for lunch.

When Nancy entered her kitchen she saw

a tuna sandwich already on the table. Next to the plate was a piece of paper.

"What's this, Hannah?" Nancy asked.

"Someone slipped a note into the mailbox about an hour ago," Hannah said. "It says something about a turkey."

"Turkey?" Nancy gasped. She stared at the note with its orange, red, and brown writing. It looked just like the last one!

"We still have the turkey and we want more candy," Nancy read out loud. "Leave another bag on your doorstep at three o'clock. P.S. We're sick of cherry lollipops!"

Nancy looked up at Hannah. "Do we have any candy in the house?" she asked.

"Just those purple candies you got for Halloween," Hannah said. "But they made your teeth turn purple, remember?"

"Perfect! They're not for me," Nancy said. "They're for the turkey thieves. And this time I'm going to catch them in the act!"

Nancy finished her lunch. Then she filled a paper bag with purple candies.

At ten minutes to three, Nancy placed the bag on her doorstep. She shut the door and climbed up on a step stool. Then she peeked out the small window on the front door. And waited . . .

Any minute now, Nancy thought. *The turkey thieves will be here and—*

"Woof, woof!"

Nancy looked over her shoulder. Chip was chewing on her math workbook!

"Chip! No!" Nancy scolded. She jumped off the step stool and grabbed the book out of Chip's mouth.

Suddenly Nancy heard a rustling noise. It sounded like it was right outside the door.

"The turkey thieves!" Nancy gasped. She ran to the door and yanked it wide open. There was no one on her doorstep. And the candy was gone!

"Phooey!" Nancy cried. "I missed them again!" She was about to go back inside when she remembered the purple candy . . .

"Someone in school will have purple teeth tomorrow," Nancy told herself. "And I'm going to find out who!"

The next morning Nancy got permission to bring her camera to school.

"You're going to take pictures of the kids

in our class?" George asked. "Why?"

"The camera has no film," Nancy whispered. "I'm just on smile patrol."

Nancy told Bess and George about the purple candies and the purple teeth.

"What if the thieves brushed their teeth this morning?" Bess asked.

"Or finished all of the candy last night?" George asked.

"No way," Nancy replied. "I gave them tons of the stuff. If they love candy that much, they probably ate some on the way to school."

The girls waited in the schoolyard for Riley. When she didn't show up they decided to get to work.

"Say cheese!" Nancy told Molly Angelo and Amara Shane.

"Cheeeeese!" the girls said.

Nancy studied their smiles as she snapped the picture. No purple teeth.

"Cheeeeeese!" Jenny March, Emily Reeves, and Kyle Leddington exclaimed.

Nancy pretended to snap a picture. No purple teeth there, either.

The girls were about to find some more

classmates when Nancy felt someone tug the back of her parka. She looked behind her and saw Lonny and Lenny Wong.

"Take our picture!" Lenny demanded. "Take our picture!"

"Go away," George told them. "You're not in our class."

"Pleeeeeease?" Lonny begged.

Nancy stared at Lonny's teeth. They were bright purple. And so were Lenny's!

7

Petting Zoo Clue

"Hey, you two!" Nancy called. "What did you do with Riley's turkey?"

Lonny and Lenny looked at each other. Then they took off through the schoolyard.

"Come back, you little pests!" George called. "And tell us where Martin is!"

Nancy's camera dangled around her neck as they chased Lonny and Lenny.

They scooted around the flagpole, see-saws, and swings. Purple candies began spilling out of Lonny's pocket.

"Hey!" a fifth-grade monitor called to the twins. "Pick all of those up!"

While the twins picked up the candies, the girls marched over.

"We gave you the candy you wanted," Nancy said. "Now where's the turkey?"

"We don't have one!" Lonny insisted.

"Except for a chocolate turkey that our grandma gave us," Lenny added. "And we ate it already."

Nancy pulled the two mysterious notes from her backpack. "Did you write these and leave them on my doorstep?" she asked.

The twins looked at each other. Then they both nodded.

"We heard you say something about a missing turkey at the Double Dip," Lenny explained.

"So we figured out a fun way to get some candy!" Lonny said with a grin.

"You mean you pretended to have a turkey?" Bess asked. "Just so we'd give you more and more candy?"

"That's the idea!" Lenny said.

"Our brother Orson wrote the notes for us," Lonny explained. "For a share of the loot."

"But he ate too much candy," Lonny

sighed. "So he's home with a tummyache."

Nancy studied the twins. "How do we know you're telling the truth?" she asked. "How do we know you don't have Martin?"

"You can come to our house and look everywhere," Lenny said with a shrug.

"Even under our beds," Lonny added. "If you can move all our dirty socks."

"Ewww!" the girls cried.

Lonny and Lenny popped more purple candies in their mouths. Then they raced toward the monkey bars.

"So much for finding the turkey thieves. I don't think those two stole Martin," Nancy decided.

"Good," Bess said. "Because I don't want to look through their dirty socks!"

The bell rang. Nancy, Bess, and George walked toward the entrance.

"We can't look for Martin after school today," Nancy said. "Hannah is taking us to the farm. Remember?"

"How could we forget?" Bess asked excitedly. "I can't wait to pet those baby goats and lambs."

"Nancy, Bess, George!" Riley called as she

ran over. "Any luck with Martin?"

"Sorry, Riley," Nancy answered. "We didn't find Martin yet."

Nancy expected Riley to look disappointed. But instead she smiled.

"That's okay," Riley said. "Let's go for some pizza after school."

"I have a better idea," Nancy said. "Why don't you come with us to a farm?"

"You bet!" Riley said. She began jumping up and down. "What farm is it?"

"It's called 'Heavenly Harvest,'" Nancy explained. "It has a petting zoo, apple cider—"

Riley stopped jumping. "I can't go," she cut in. "I just remembered. I promised my mom . . . that I'd . . . water our plants!"

"We can wait until you finish your chores," Nancy offered.

"I can't go!" Riley said again. She turned and ran way ahead of them.

"What was her problem?" George asked.

Nancy shook her head. "I may be a detective," she said. "But I don't have a clue!"

* * * *

"Welcome to Heavenly Harvest!" a woman with twinkling green eyes said. "I'm Hattie and this is my husband, Hank. We own the whole place."

"It's awesome!" Nancy gasped.

She looked around the farm and smiled. A big red barn stood in the distance. Near it was a pen filled with small animals. Market stalls sold cider, pies, vegetables, and colorful Indian corn.

Hank and Hattie looked like real farmers in plaid shirts and overalls.

"All of our visitors get to wear these little pins," Hattie told them.

As Hattie dropped a silver pin into each of their hands, Nancy couldn't believe her eyes. They were *cow* pins!

"Enjoy the farm!" Hank said. He and Hattie gave a little wave as they left to greet other visitors.

Nancy pulled out the silver pin they had found in Riley's yard. She quickly compared it to the new cow pin Hattie had just given her.

"It's a match!" Nancy declared.

"Maybe Riley came to this farm once too," George said. "And got a pin."

"But Riley said she never saw the cow pin in her life," Nancy remembered.

"She also said she didn't like cows," Bess said. She shook her head. "Who doesn't like cows?"

"Okay, girls," Hannah said. "Speaking of animals, how about that petting zoo?"

The girls fastened the pins to their jackets. Then they raced ahead of Hannah to the animal pen.

"I see calves!" Nancy called out as they neared the pen.

"I see a llama!" George said.

"I think I see a turkey!" Bess said.

"A turkey?" Nancy asked. She leaned over the fence and peered into the pen. Strutting around a bucket of feed was a big turkey.

"Gobble, gobble!" it screeched.

Nancy gasped. The turkey had a black feathery beard on his chest with a red feather in the middle!

"Bess, George—look at that turkey!" Nancy gasped. "Could it be . . . ?"

8

Lies and Pumpkin Pies

It is!" George declared. "It's Martin!"

"What's he doing here?" Bess asked.

Nancy began putting the pieces together. "Riley said that her aunt and uncle owned a farm," she said. "Which is where they kept Martin."

"Nancy!" Bess gasped. "Do you think her aunt and uncle are Hank and Hattie?"

"There's only one way to find out," Nancy said. "Let's ask them!"

While Hannah bought some corn and squash, the girls looked for Hank and Hattie. They found them inside a stall setting up jars of jellies and mustards.

"Excuse me," Nancy said. "But do you know a girl named Riley McArthur?"

Hank and Hattie both smiled.

"Riley is our niece," Hattie replied. "How do you know her?"

"Riley's in our class," Nancy explained. "Last Friday she told us that Martin, the turkey, was missing."

"Missing?" Hattie chuckled. "Why, he's in the pen right now!"

"Sure!" Hank said. "We picked him up last Friday like we said we would."

"He gobbled all the way home!" Hattie said. "Must have been gosh darn homesick!"

Nancy stared at Bess and George. So the turkey in the pen *was* Martin!

"You must have lost this pin, too," Nancy said. She handed the cow pin to Hattie. "We found it in Riley's backyard on Saturday."

"So that's where I dropped it!" Hattie exclaimed. She reached out and took the pin. Then the couple got back to work.

As the girls walked away from the stall, Nancy shook her head. "Riley made the whole thing up," she said. "Why would she do that?"

She saw Hannah waving to them from a nearby pumpkin patch.

"Come on, you three!" Hannah called. "Help me pick out the perfect pumpkin for my pie!"

The girls ran to join Hannah. They had fun pumpkin picking, drinking apple cider, and climbing bales of hay.

When it was time to leave, Nancy asked Hannah to drop them off at Riley's house.

Riley smiled at the girls when she opened the front door. But when she saw their pins, her face turned chalk white.

"W-Wow," Riley stammered. "Those pins look just like—"

"The one we found in your backyard," George cut in. "Yeah, we know."

Riley's eyes lowered to the ground. "So I guess you saw Martin at the farm, huh?" she asked.

"We saw him, all right," Nancy told Riley. "He was never missing, was he?"

"No," Riley sighed. "I guess I sort of . . . lied."

"Why?" Bess wanted to know.

Riley looked straight at Nancy. "Because

you're a detective," she said. "That's why!"

"What does that have to do with anything?" Nancy asked.

"After Brenda made me leave the table last week I thought I'd never make new friends in River Heights," Riley explained. "So I got you to solve a mystery. So we could spend lots of time together like real friends!"

Nancy felt badly for Riley. All she wanted were new friends. But did she have to lie?

"We were going to be your friends anyway, Riley," Nancy admitted.

"But now that you lied to us," George told Riley, "I'm not sure I want to be your friend."

"Me neither," Bess agreed. "What if you keep lying to us?"

"I promise I won't," Riley said. "I hated lying about Martin. But I didn't know what else to do."

"All you had to do was be nice," Nancy suggested. "You would have made lots of new friends that way."

Riley's shoulders dropped.

"Does this mean we'll *never* be friends?" she asked.

Nancy glanced at Bess and George. They stepped away from the doorstep, huddled together, and began to whisper.

"Riley did finally tell us the truth," Nancy said.

"She could have kept on lying," Bess pointed out. "But she didn't."

"And she does great cartwheels," George added. "I think we should give Riley another chance."

"Me too," Nancy whispered.

"Me three," Bess whispered.

The girls turned back to Riley.

"Of course we'll be your friends, Riley," Nancy said with a smile.

"All right!" Riley cheered. "Does this mean we can go to the movies? And ice-skating? And sleep-overs?"

"Why don't you start by coming to my house on Thanksgiving afternoon?" Nancy asked. "For a piece of pumpkin pie."

"Wow!" Riley exclaimed. "Are you sure you want to invite me, Nancy?"

"Sure I'm sure," Nancy replied. "That's what friends are for!"

* * * *

Thanksgiving Day couldn't come fast enough for Nancy. When it finally did, she and Riley ate pie, played board games, and told turkey jokes.

But while Riley romped around with Chocolate Chip, Nancy had important work to do. She opened her notebook, turned to a clean page, and began to write.

If Thanksgiving is for giving thanks, I'm thankful for a ton of things. I'm thankful that I solved the case and found Martin safe and sound. But most of all, I'm thankful for Daddy, Hannah, Bess, George, and my puppy, Chip. And I'm thankful for brand-new friends— like Riley McArthur!

CASE CLOSED

THIRD-GRADE DETECTIVES

Everyone in the third grade loves the new teacher, Mr. Merlin.

Mr. Merlin used to be a spy, and he knows all about secret codes and the strange and gross ways the police solve mysteries.

YOU CAN HELP DECODE THE CLUES AND SOLVE THE MYSTERY IN THESE OTHER STORIES ABOUT THE THIRD-GRADE DETECTIVES:

#1 The Clue of the Left-handed Envelope

#2 The Puzzle of the Pretty Pink Handkerchief

#3 The Mystery of the Hairy Tomatoes

#4 The Cobweb Confession

#5 The Riddle of the Stolen Sand

Coming Soon: #6 The Secret of the Green Skin

Ready-for-Chapters